This book belongs to:

_____

I am 3

Yippee!

Make a Match

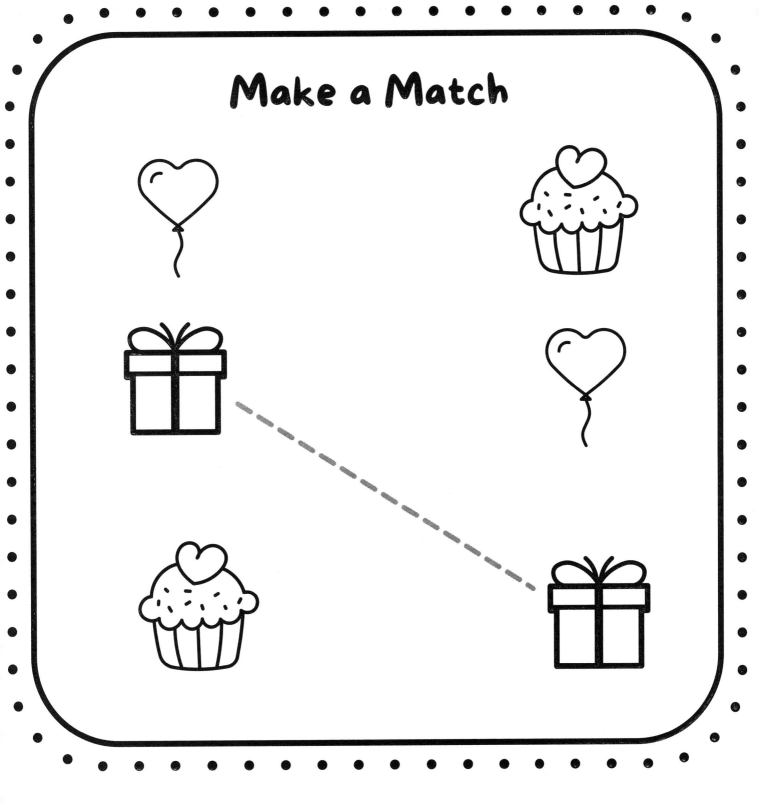

Count and Match

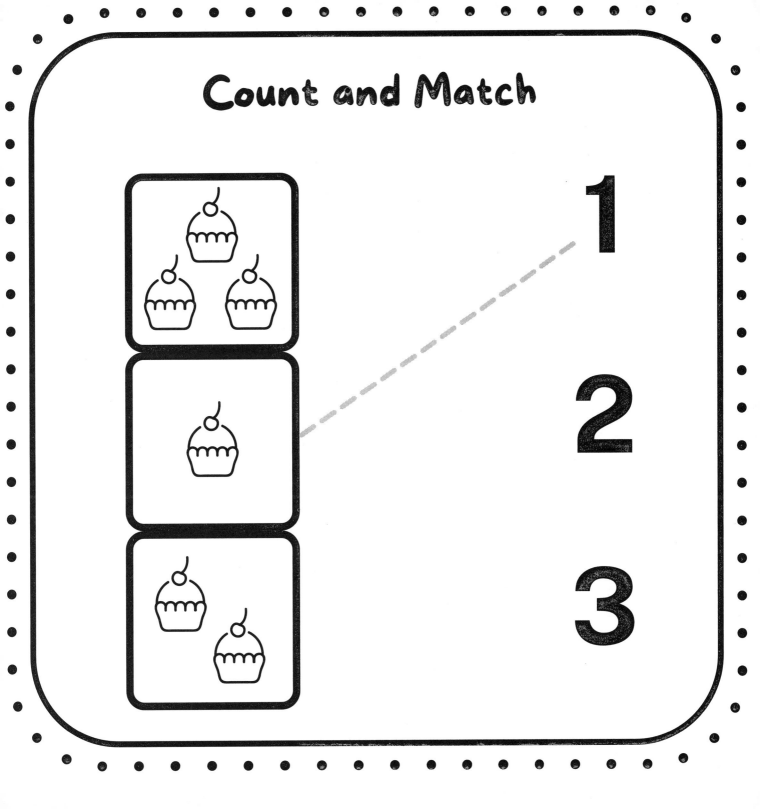

Find 3

Trace the lines to help the friends find their toys.

Count and Color

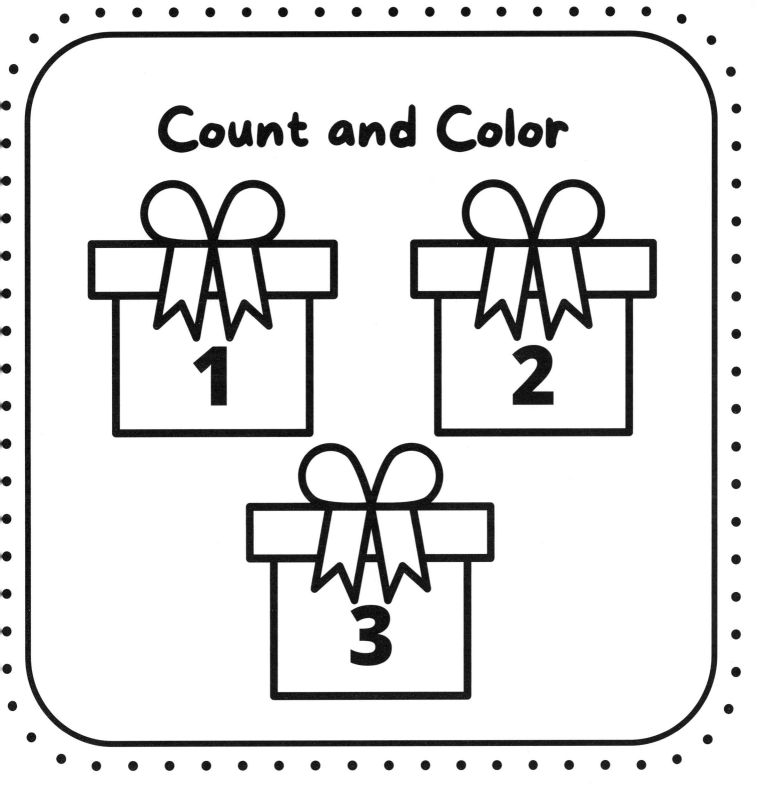

Rainbow write the number 3.
Trace the number with 3 colors.

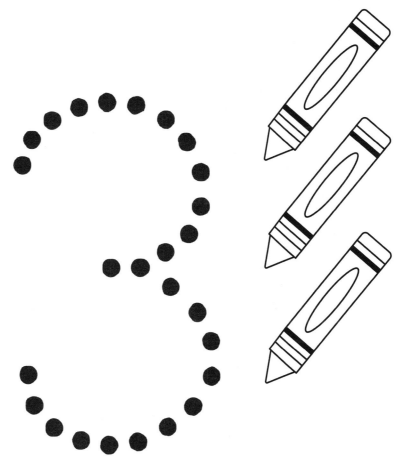

Make a Match

Trace the numbers.
Match the number to the butterflies.

1 2 3

Go through the maze to get all 3 cupcakes.

I can draw

Trace the circle and draw a happy face.

Find 3

Count and Match

1

2

3

Follow the trail to help the friends get their treats.

Go through the maze to get all 3 ladybugs.

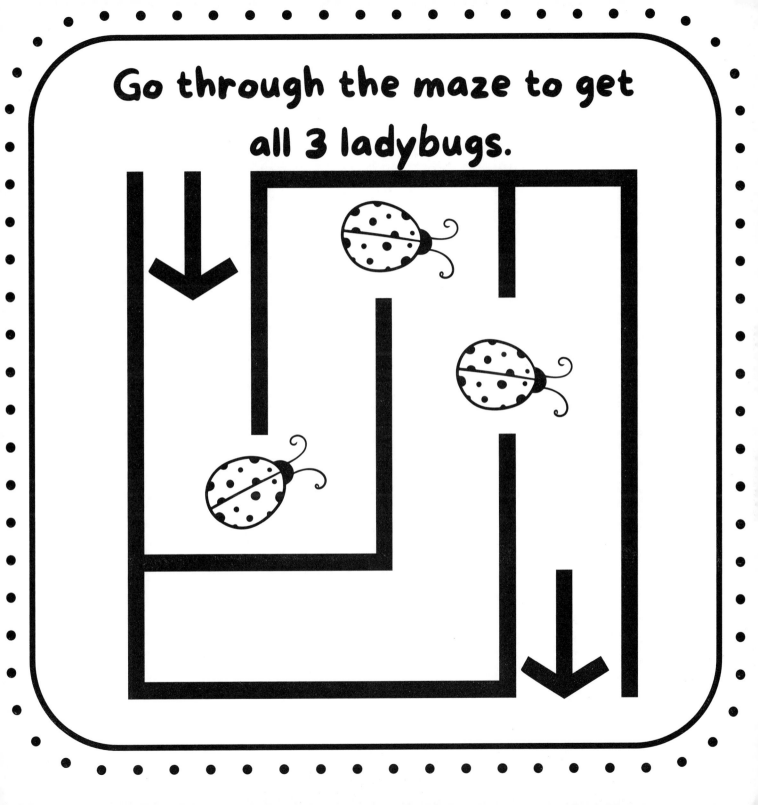

I am 3

I can draw a picture.

1